George Washington's Cows

George Washington's Cows
❧ David Small ❧

Farrar Straus Giroux

New York

To Sarah and Mark

Special thanks to the Mount Vernon Ladies Association

Copyright © 1994 by David Small. All rights reserved. Distributed in Canada by Douglas & McIntyre Ltd. Color separations by Hong Kong Scanner Craft. Printed and bound in Singapore. Designed by Lilian Rosenstreich. First edition, 1994.
15 14 13 10 9 8 7 6 5

Library of Congress Cataloging-in-Publication Data. Small, David. George Washington's cows/ David Small. — 1st ed. p.   em.   [1. Washington, George, 1732–1799—Fiction. 2. Domestic animals—Fiction. 3. Stories in rhyme.] I. Title. PZ8.3.S634Ge 1994 [E]—dc20 93-39989

George Washington's cows were kept upstairs
And given their own special room.

They never were seen by the light of day,
No matter for what or by whom.

They had to be dressed in lavender gowns
and bedded on cushions of silk,

Fed on a diet of jam and cream scones,
Frequently sprayed with expensive colognes,
Begged every hour in obsequious tones,
Or they just wouldn't give any milk.

George Washington's hogs, on the other hand,
Were a genteel and amiable group,

Delighted to help with the household chores
If a servant had fever or croup.

They served the dinner precisely at eight
With manners uncommonly fine.

Eager to serve the honored guests,
Leaping to meet each need expressed,
Always polite and impeccably dressed,
They were certainly well-bred swine.

George Washington's sheep were all scholars,
With a flock of impressive degrees.

They had not the least bit of trouble
In counting to twenty by threes.

They sorted the stars with a needle
And measured the sea with a stick.

Then, raising their hoofs in triumph, they cried:
"We say with a certain amount of pride,
If the ocean were stood up on its side
You would see that it's deep but not thick!"

With head in hand, George Washington sighed
And shed a few tears in his tea.

"My cows wear dresses, my pigs wear wigs,
And my sheep are more learnèd than me.
In all my days on the farm I've seen
Nothing to equal such tricks."

Then bundling into his wool underwear,
He ferried across the cold Delaware,
And muttered in tones of deepest despair: